GW00818698

5-Minute JUNGLE TALES for Bedtime

Illustrated by Peter Stevenson

Stories by Carolyn Adlington, Catherine Bald, David Kremer, Geoffrey Cowan, Nicola Kremer, Wendy Hobson, Joanne Hanks, Vivienne Frow, Barbara Matthews, Fran Pickering, Gail Rose, Tim L. West, Anne Sharples, Julie West, Kim Kremer and Jenny Walters.

DEAN

Editor: Kim Kremer
Editorial Assistant: Joanne Hanks
Production: Mark Leonard

Illustrated by Peter Stevenson

Stories by Wendy Hobson, Fran Pickering,
Geoffrey Cowan, David Kremer, Barbara Matthews,
Julie West, Catherine Bald, Jennie Walters, Kim Kremer,
Vivienne Frow, Joanne Hanks, Tim L. West, Carolyn Adlington,
Gail Rose, Nicola Kremer, Anne Sharples

This edition published in 1995 by Dean,
an imprint of Reed International Books Limited,
Michelin House, 81 Fulham Road, London SW3 6RB,
and Auckland, Melbourne, Singapore and Toronto.

Copyright © 1995 Reed International Books Limited

ISBN 0 603 55411 3

British Library Cataloguing-in-Publication Data
A catalogue record for this book is available from the British Library.

Printed in Great Britain

M r & Mrs Longneck kept their important things in a very high cupboard in the bathroom where young Leonard Longneck couldn't reach them.

Leonard, being a curious giraffe, wished he could reach the cupboard so that he could see the treasures he imagined lay within.

One day, while his parents were busy in the kitchen, Leonard balanced the clothes basket on top of the bathroom stool and climbed up to peer into the cupboard.

But the door was shut tight!

Leonard pulled and pulled, but the door wouldn't budge. Leonard gave one last tremendous heave, and the door flew open. Leonard fell to the floor with a crash, grazing his knee.

Mrs Longneck rushed in to see Leonard rubbing at his sore knee.

'What on earth have you done?' she asked.

'I wanted to see the treasure in the cupboard,' Leonard replied.

'There's no treasure in there,' sighed Mrs Longneck, reaching into the cupboard and taking out plasters and ointment. 'Just these.' That was lucky for Leonard, since his knee was hurting by this time and the plasters and ointment felt like treasure as they soothed the pain.

I t was the night before the Jungle Birds' Choir put on an open-air concert for all the other creatures.

Young Tommy Toucan had to sing a solo. He went to bed early to get plenty of rest, but as he peered out into the darkness, he saw lots of bright lights.

'They're only friendly fireflies!' his mummy said when he called her.

Mummy explained that fireflies were really flying beetles with glowing light-spots on them.

On the night of the concert, the audience began to file in and take their seats by the stage, all chattering noisily. But just as the choir was about to sing the first note, all the stage lights went out.

'Whatever shall we do?' asked Helen Hummingbird.

Tommy Toucan wasn't going to sing in the dark – it was his big night and he wanted to be seen. 'Fetch the fireflies!' he told his mother. And that is just what she did. The Jungle Birds' Choir sang under hundreds of flitting 'spotlights', and everyone agreed that it was their best concert ever.

The little boa constrictors surrounded the large, old snake who was curled up asleep in the hollow of a tree.

'Tell us the story about your jungle journey, Grandpa,' they said, waking him from a pleasant dream.

'It was a long time ago,' he began. 'I set off to find the hidden temple on the other side of the jungle. First I travelled far through the undergrowth towards the rising sun, never stopping for a rest or a snack. As the sun rose high, I changed direction, circling round in great loops to cover my tracks.'

'Who would be following, Grandpa?' asked the smallest boa, but Grandpa didn't stop to answer.

'Finally,' he continued, 'I went up and made my way along the tree branches – up and along, up and along – to give me a view of the way ahead . . .'

The little ones watched with delight as the old snake stopped short – always at the same point in the tale. For as he spoke, he followed the route of his adventure, winding himself round the branches of the tree, stretching and curling until he tied himself into a huge knot! Then the giggling snakes had to untie him and settle him down for a rest! They never did find out if he found the temple, but it was still their favourite story.

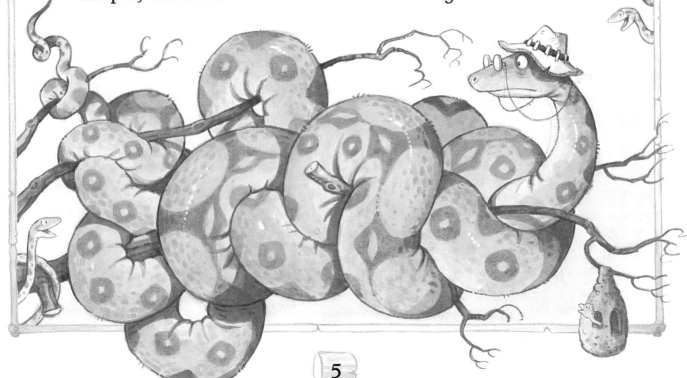

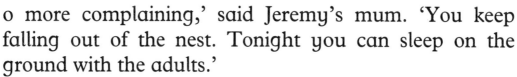

No more complaining,' said Jeremy's mum. 'You keep falling out of the nest. Tonight you can sleep on the ground with the adults.'

'But I don't want to sleep down there,' Jeremy persisted. 'It's not as warm and cosy on the ground.'

'Nonsense,' replied his mother. 'It's very soft.'

'Can't I make my own nest?' begged Jeremy.

'If you want to,' his mum replied doubtfully, 'but you won't be as comfortable.'

Jeremy worked at his high tree nest all afternoon. That night, he snuggled down, wriggling to make himself comfortable.

A twig stuck in his back. A leafy branch poked in his ear. He shuffled again, rocking the nest. And finally, after more wriggling, he fell right out of the nest and into a patch of ferns.

As he began to climb back into the tree, he noticed how soft the ferns were. Without thinking, he pulled a few around him, rested his head on a pile of leaves and drifted quickly back to sleep.

'Did you fall out of your nest last night?' his mum asked with a smile when he woke up next morning.

'Oh no,' said Jeremy. 'I decided I would rather sleep on the ground after all!'

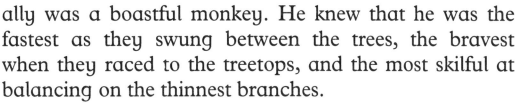

Wally was a boastful monkey. He knew that he was the fastest as they swung between the trees, the bravest when they raced to the treetops, and the most skilful at balancing on the thinnest branches.

'I can go the highest,' boasted Wally one day. 'I can even climb that thin branch.' The monkeys gasped 'You couldn't!' they cried. But Wilma was fed up with Wally's boasting. She had noticed that he had grown fatter since the last race.

'Race you up there!' she said.

The two monkeys sped off up the branches. Quick as a flash, Wally had reached the skinny branch on the tree top. 'I won!' he cried to the others below. But the branch began to crack . . . Wally couldn't climb off in time, and as the branch broke and fell, he tumbled down with it, crashing through leaves and branches. Wilma caught hold of the end of his tail as he fell. 'Ouch!' he cried, as he dangled a few feet above the ground. The monkeys cheered – Wilma had saved his life, and Wally never boasted again.

W henever anyone wanted to know anything, such as where they had left their keys, or when a birthday was, they only had to ask Albert the elephant. Because Albert, like any elephant, had an amazing memory. He quite simply never forgot.

But one day, Albert did forget. He was just taking a stroll through the jungle, when suddenly, a falling coconut landed on his head. Albert began to see stars . . . Peregrine Monkey saw it happen. He did think it was funny, but he said, 'Albert? Are you all right?'

'Who's Albert?' said Albert the elephant. Poor Albert couldn't even remember his name! He couldn't remember where he lived, what his friends' names were, or even why he had a trunk!

His friends were very worried about him. It was Peregrine who said, 'Well, if a coconut can make him *lose* his memory, perhaps it can help him *find* it again too!'

The animals decided to give it a try. Peregrine climbed a tall tree with a large coconut, and dropped it on Albert's head. Albert was *very* cross. 'Peregrine Monkey!' he cried. 'I could have lost my memory with a blow like that!'

Albert was his old self again!

The animals chattered excitedly one morning as they gathered for school.

'What do you think the new teacher will be like?' they asked, scurrying about, too excited to sit in their places.

'Let's draw a picture of him on the blackboard,' said one of the cheekier monkeys, 'and see if it looks like him!' With an orange chalk, he drew a large, hairy face. His friend filled in a wide, toothy grin and a sagging double chin. The others added a pot-belly, long hairy arms, and huge feet.

The class stood back, giggling, to admire their work, when a low voice made them jump.

'Good morning, children.' The animals gasped and rushed back to their places.

The teacher walked to the front of the class, swaying slightly on his big feet, his long hairy arms hanging beside him and his big pot belly sticking out in front. He looked at the picture and his mouth spread into a wide, toothy grin.

'Well, children,' he said proudly, 'What a fetching portrait of me!'

And the animals knew at once that they would get on well with their new school teacher.

Betty Bat's mother said she should have been called Batty because she always did such crazy things.

Once, Betty decided that she was bored with eating fruit and was going to hunt insects instead. She ended up with a dreadful stomach ache.

Another time, Betty tried sleeping rightside up like other animals, instead of upside down. It was very difficult to balance. She fell off the branch when she was half-asleep, and landed on her head!

It was Betty who hung too near the end of the branch to see if it would hold her weight – and ended up with bruises all over her body when the branch snapped, and she fell to the ground.

So it came as quite a surprise to everyone when Betty announced that she was going to try to be a sensible bat. Then she flew off to find a meal just as the sun was rising above the jungle and all the other bats were just settling down to sleep!

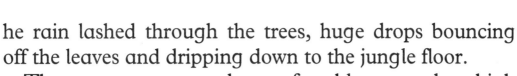

The rain lashed through the trees, huge drops bouncing off the leaves and dripping down to the jungle floor.

The parrots roosted comfortably on the high branches. The leopards and tigers were nowhere to be seen, hiding away until the rainstorm passed. The python was curled snugly in a tree hollow, eyes closed.

But suddenly a whoop of delight and a flurry of activity rocked the python from his slumber and made him curl down his head and flick out his tongue to find out what was going on. There were swishing and splashing sounds, sliding and slurping noises, loud chatterings and giggles.

And what he saw made his snake eyes widen even further. For down below him was a bustle of the brightest and jolliest tree frogs he had ever seen. Amidst hoots of joy, they were sliding down a huge waterchute which they had made by lashing together a spiral of the biggest, most slippery leaves. They slid down, helter-skelter, landing with a tremendous splash in a muddy mess on the jungle floor.

'Children!' sighed the snake, curling back to sleep with a wide yawn. 'I slide down slippery slopes every day, and I never make such a fuss about it!'

The monkey troop had just moved to a new patch of the jungle and the youngsters were exploring.

'Hey, look at this!' cried Jessie to her brother and sister. Growing on a tree trunk, was the largest flower the monkeys had ever seen. It had great brown and white spots, and it smelt TERRIBLE!

Simon grinned wickedly. 'We can use it as a stinkbomb!' And that is what they did. Before long, the whole neighbourhood began to complain about an odd smell. When the chimps got home, Mum said, 'Into the bath with the lot of you! You smell awful!'

The chimps groaned, as Mum scrubbed behind their ears. Of course, even when the children were sparkling clean, the smell didn't go away. 'Hmm,' said Mum. 'Maybe I didn't wash you well enough . . .'

'No!' cried the chimps, and they told her about how they had used the flower as a stinkbomb – anything was better than another bath. Mum was very cross. She made them scrub clean every nest in the street. 'That flower is called a Rafflesia, and you are never to touch it again!' she said.

'We won't!' wailed the chimps, as they polished and scrubbed.

Peter was certainly a friend it was a little hard to get close to. You could nuzzle his nose quite safely, but to approach him from any other angle was not a good idea. For Peter was a porcupine. What's more he was a very large and round porcupine for his age.

He was also a very friendly and helpful chap. If Peter noticed someone struggling with their shopping, he would rush up to help. But so many animals had dropped their bags and parcels in fright, that it rather put him off.

Then Mrs Armadillo came to the rescue. Peter's appearance did not bother her. She hung all her bags from the spikes on his back, and everyone could see how useful he could be.

After that, Peter was never short of people who needed his help. In fact, he was in great demand as the best shopping carrier in the jungle.

The baby crocodiles liked nothing better than to swim in the river, while their mother watched lazily from the bank, or slid into the water for a cooling dip.

Harry was particularly adventurous. In fact, his mother complained that he was too adventurous because he often swam right out into the swift-flowing river and was carried downstream. Then one of the adults had to rescue him and bring him back to safety. They always told him off.

'You are a foolish crocodile,' they nagged. 'One of these days, you'll float off right down the river and never come back.' But he always smiled broadly because it really was such fun!

But one day, he went too far. When he had been rescued for the fourth time, Grandpa, the oldest and the largest crocodile, decided he had had enough. He waded downstream into the river and stuck his great feet into the mud, making a barrier across the water.

'Now you can't go any further,' he said, 'and we can have a rest!'

But do you know, it was just as much fun floating down the current and bumping into Grandpa as it was floating further downstream. So everyone was happy.

W here shall I hide?' David the little shrew, muttered as he scampered about the undergrowth on the jungle floor. He could hear the others slowly counting up to 50 . . . He had to find a good hiding place.

As he turned round for the umpteenth time, a beautiful bird of paradise flew down and rested on a branch. His magnificent tail cascaded on the ground.

'That's it!' said David, rushing to hide himself.

'Coming!' came the cry, and shrews darted in all directions. The bird looked at David.

'Can I be of any assistance?' he asked.

'Yes, please,' whispered David. 'First they have to find me and then join me in my hiding place. But there's not enough room.'

'Just leave it to me,' said the bird.

Christopher's face popped between the feathers.

'There you are,' he said. 'Not much room here!'

'Allow me!' said the bird of paradise and spread his tail, fan-like, a little further.

'Found you!' cried Melissa. 'Bit of a squeeze!'

'Allow me!' said the bird of paradise, again spreading his tail feathers to hide them perfectly.

By the end of the game, all the shrews were huddled together under the colourful canopy of feathers. What a wonderful game! And everyone said that David's hiding place was the best one ever.

Tony Toucan was vain. He liked to sit preening his feathers, polishing his beak or gazing at himself in a pool. When his friends asked him to play hide-and-seek or tag, he would say,

'No, I might ruffle my feathers.'

One day, Tony's friend Tricia had an idea. There had been a rainstorm and the jungle was muddy and wet.

'Fly down to the river with me,' she said. 'We can stop at every puddle, if you like.' So off they flew, chatting happily. As they flew to the first pool, some mud splashed on Tony's legs, but he was looking at his face, so he didn't notice.

At the second, his wing dipped in the muddy water, but he was admiring his beak so he didn't notice. At the third pool, his face was splattered with mud, but Tricia shouted, 'Oh, look at that wonderful flower,' to distract his attention, and he didn't notice.

Finally they reached the river, but before Tony could look at his reflection, Tricia said,

'Haven't we had a lovely morning?' Tony looked down in surprise at the mud-splattered bird gazing at him from the water, but somehow it didn't matter that he looked a mess.

'Yes,' he said, smiling, 'We have!'

Cedric was a very small flying squirrel with three spots on his left wrist, and two spots on his right wrist. Cedric was a terrible flier and he wished that he could be less clumsy. When the other squirrels leapt out to glide across the air from tree to tree, they landed exactly where they wanted. But Cedric landed with a bump into the tree trunk. The trouble was that Cedric didn't know his right from his left. When his mother shouted, 'Left arm forward!' Cedric moved his right arm. And when she shouted, 'Right leg down!' Cedric moved his left.

'What are we going to do with you?' his mother would say, shaking her head in despair, after a disastrous gliding lesson. Cedric's brother had an idea.

'He can use his spots as a code!' he cried. Of course, Cedric had no trouble remembering his spots. 'Three spots forward!' meant his left arm, and 'Two spots back!' meant his right. After that, it was all plain sailing.

It was the middle of the day, the sun was shining, and Brenda the bushbaby couldn't sleep.

'It always sounds so exciting in the jungle in the daytime,' she thought. 'Why do we bushbabies miss all the fun by sleeping in the day and coming out at night?' Brenda was curious. Carefully, so that she did not wake the family, Brenda climbed out of the nest.

A snuffling and scurrying in the undergrowth made her jump. It was a large bony armadillo wandering past. A loud screeching sound and a great flapping of wings startled her and made her cling tightly to the tree. It was a family of brightly-coloured parrots flying by. A rocking of the branches and a chittering and chattering sent her rushing back towards the hole. It was a troop of mischievous monkeys playing games. Brenda climbed quickly back into the hole and snuggled down again next to her mother.

'I think it is much too exciting in the jungle in the daytime,' she said as she went back to sleep. 'I'll come out again at night.'

The sloth family had decided to go on an outing. In fact, it took them all week to decide to go on an outing, because it took them so long to do *anything.*

The morning of the outing arrived, and the family lazily began to gather in the branches.

'I'll just have a look around,' Dad said, 'to make sure it's a good day to go.' He set off, moving his hands in slow motion as he hung under the branch. The others waited patiently, munching slowly on a leaf, swaying and dozing a little as they hung there. They were in no hurry. Finally, Dad returned.

'It's a good day for an outing,' he announced. 'Now which way were we going to go?'

This caused a problem, for none of them could remember. As it reached mid-day and they began to get hungry, they decided to eat lunch before setting off.

After lunch, they thought they'd have a little nap. They spread out in the tree and dozed happily in the warmth. By the time they woke up, the sun was beginning to drop in the sky.

'It's a bit late to set off now,' said Dad. 'Perhaps we had better go another day.'

'We can think about it tomorrow,' said Mum.

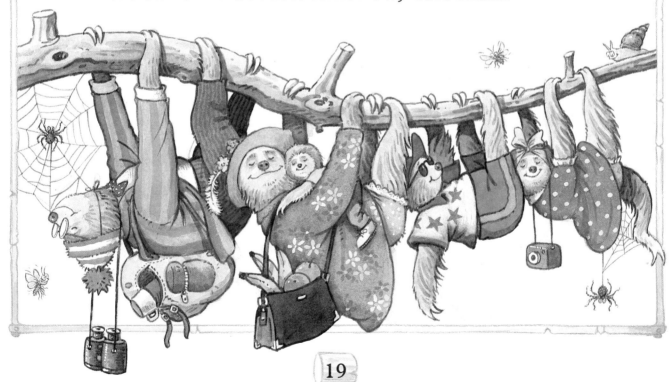

The old parrot sat unhappily on a branch. A shaft of sunlight cut through the leaves and shone fiercely on her feathered head.

'It's too hot,' she squawked, and shuffled along the branch back into the shade.

'Not feeling well today, Rosie?' asked Sam, a bright blue and red parrot, flying over to land on the branch. 'You look very dull in the feathers.'

As the leaves moved, another ray of sun shone brightly on Rosie's curved beak. She squinted and moved again along the branch.

'No,' she murmured sadly. 'I'm all hot and bothered.'

'I'll soon have you sorted out,' said Sam.

Sam flew off and when he returned, he was followed by a flock of tiny hummingbirds. Rosie was mystified, but only for a moment. The hummingbirds flew around her and hovered in a circle. Humming quietly, the rapid beats of their wings fanned cool air all around Rosie and made her feel cooler for the first time that day.

'Oh, Sam, what an excellent idea,' said Rosie. 'Now I know I shall feel better in no time.'

One year Little Tusker Elephant decided to spend the summer living by the river at the edge of the jungle. He built himself a cosy house and then looked round for a few friends. Everyone likes friends to chat to.

However most of the other creatures seemed rather afraid of him and ran away when he came thud-thud-thudding along on his big, round feet.

Then one day, a deer noticed Little Tusker sucking water up from the river and squirting it over his back.

'That's a very useful thing to be able to do,' she said. 'Would you squirt water over my youngsters for me, please? They certainly need cleaning.'

Little Tusker was happy to give the young deer a wash. And they loved the water squiggling all over them. Word spread and soon lots of the animals were coming for a shower and of course a gossip. Before long, Little Tusker had lots of friends. Knowing how to do something useful is a good way to get to know people.

Rainbow sat on a branch, feeling lonely. He swivelled his eyes around and caught sight of his uncle resting in the leaves above him.

'Hello, Uncle,' said Rainbow, climbing up to him. 'There are lots of flies by that big flower on the jungle floor. Come down and have lunch with me.'

'Not hungry, son,' muttered his uncle, and slithered away. His cousin Charlie was standing by a flower so Rainbow made his way down to join him.

'Hello, Charlie,' said Rainbow happily. 'Mind if I share your lunch?'

'I prefer to eat alone,' Charlie grunted.

Rainbow knew when he was not wanted. He walked off sadly. Then he heard a rustle and a sniff. A frog was sitting in a puddle on a leaf.

'Hello,' said Rainbow. 'You look down in the mouth.' The frog gulped loudly.

'I'm not like the other frogs,' he complained. 'They are happy on their own but I want someone to talk to.'

'Why, so do I!' said Rainbow happily. 'Where do you come from? Would you like some lunch? What's your name, by the way?' And the pair walked happily off, chatting about this, that and five dozen other things to their hearts' content.

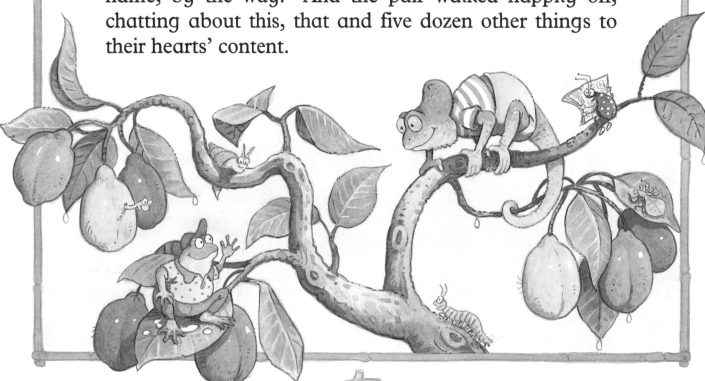

Thomas played happily on the bank of the river chasing butterflies while the rest of his family lazed along the banks, keeping cool in the lapping water.

'Come and cool down,' said his dad. 'It's lovely.' But Thomas would not set foot in the river. Unlike all the other tigers, he hated the water.

Just then, Thomas spotted the biggest, most brightly coloured butterfly he had ever seen. He leapt in the air, batting at it with his paws. The butterfly darted this way and that with Thomas following behind.

He was concentrating so hard on the butterfly that he did not notice when his back paws dipped into the water as he ran along, and his tail swished great splashes into the air; or when he landed with a great splosh in the shallows after an especially high leap. When the little butterfly fluttered away from the river Thomas was wet from nose to tail.

'You can hardly say you don't like the water now,' said his dad. Thomas looked at himself – covered in glistening drops.

'Isn't it nice and cool in the river!' his dad laughed.

The parrots had wings and could fly anywhere. Sometimes, they flew for miles to explore the jungle and still came back in time for tea.

Old Grandma Parrot had explored wondrous lands in her day. She had a good memory as well. When any of the little monkeys could not get to sleep at night, Mummy Monkey used to send for Grandma Parrot to tell them a story. Their favourite stories were about her adventures at sea when she sailed with pirates and perched on the Captain's shoulder.

'We used to have fights at sea in our sailing ships,' squawked Grandma Parrot. 'We stole chests full of gold and buried them on a desert island, marking the place with a cross.'

'Is it still there? Will you show us how to find it?' the little monkeys would ask.

But Grandma Parrot would just laugh. 'When you are grown up and can fly, I will,' she said.

Of course the little monkeys never did learn to fly even though they practised every day, and the treasure is probably there still, waiting to be found.

Slinky the snake liked living in the jungle. He never bothered to go to school. He thought school was no fun at all. What was fun was slithering up and down trees all day. The best game was crawling to the end of a branch where it was as thin as could be and hanging there, swinging in the wind. But one day Slinky went on to a branch that was too thin, or Slinky was too fat. Whichever it was, the branch broke and Slinky fell down, down, down into the muddy river.

Slinky couldn't swim. He coughed and choked, struggled and wriggled and at last climbed out of the river.

How the other animals laughed!

Now if only Slinky had bothered to go to school, he might have learned how to swim.

My favourite spot is down by the edge of a little waterhole I know,' said Walter Warthog. 'Then I can enjoy a nice mud-bath!'

'Ooh! It sounds very sticky!' replied Cherry Chimp. 'My favourite spot is up in a big, shady tree!'

Soon some other animals arrived and each of them thought of their favourite spot.

'Mine is among some lush grass, by the river,' said Brett Buffalo dreamily.

'I know a nice rocky spot where I can sit and see for miles,' said Bessie Baboon.

So it went on as, one after another, the animals spoke up. When it came to Oscar Ostrich's turn, he looked quite puzzled. 'The trouble is I have lots of favourite spots,' he said.

'Where are they?' asked Walter.

The others waited for Oscar to answer. Suddenly, he pointed to someone running to join them.

'Here they come now!' replied Oscar. 'See? They're on Chas Cheetah's fur. They must be my favourite spots because he's my favourite friend!'

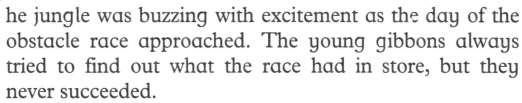

The jungle was buzzing with excitement as the day of the obstacle race approached. The young gibbons always tried to find out what the race had in store, but they never succeeded.

'We have one last chance to sneak a look!' Monty whispered to his friends. 'And I have a plan.' He had made a cloak of leaves which he threw over his head. 'They'll never spot me in this disguise,' he boasted as he set off. The trouble was it was rather difficult to see out of the leafy cloak, and rather difficult to tread quietly when he couldn't see where he was going. When he could almost see the obstacle course, one of the sentries slowly swung towards him.

'Look, George,' he called to a friend, 'here's a nice bunch of leaves. Let's stop for a break.' With a sly wink, the two sat next to Monty and began picking leaves from his cloak. Poor Monty sat frozen to the spot as his disguise slowly disappeared. Finally, George lifted the leaf that hid Monty's face.

'Why, Monty!' he cried in pretended surprise. 'What on earth are you doing here?' Monty did not wait to answer; he fled. The two old gibbons laughed.

'I could have told him that trick wouldn't work,' laughed George. 'I tried it when I was his age!'

Lizzie Leopard had a skipping-rope. She practised with it until she could skip forwards, backwards, do double-skips and even triple-skips!

One afternoon, Rory Rhinoceros saw her.

'I wish I could skip,' he sighed.

'I'll teach you!' replied Lizzie.

Rory borrowed the skipping-rope and started to skip. THUD-KER-THUD! THUMPETY-THUD!

Lizzie had forgotten how very heavy Rory was. As he jumped up and down, the ground shook so much that Lizzie's dad bounced out of his garden chair.

Indoors, things fell off shelves and tables and the whole house vibrated.

'Stop!' Lizzie's mum called to Rory from the window, but he did not hear. Then the skipping-rope caught on his foot and Rory tumbled to the ground with one last KER-THUD!

'I think that's enough practice for now,' said Lizzie.

A few days later, Rory passed her home again.

'Can I have another go with your skipping-rope, please?' he asked.

Lizzie led Rory into the back garden to show him her new trampoline.

'Why not use that instead?' she smiled. 'With luck, this time, nothing else will bounce about but you!'

THE JUST RIGHT HOUSE

The Monkey family lived in a cosy house Grandpa and Grandma had built, three quarters of the way up a very tall tree.

'This house is in just the right place,' they said. 'Just high enough to be safe from dangerous leopards, and low enough to be sheltered from the wind.'

But the young monkeys wanted to live where they could see the sky. They built themselves another house at the top of the tree.

'When I was a little chap, my great grandpa told me that once there was such a strong wind that it blew away all the houses at the tops of the trees,' said Grandpa.

The young monkeys laughed and said that strong winds like that did not blow any more – if ever they had!

But one day, a strong wind did blow. It blew the new house to pieces and the young monkeys were glad to climb down to the Just Right House, all safe and sound three quarters of the way up a very tall tree.

Mary Monkey was getting worried. She was looking for her naughty little baby, Maurice, and she couldn't see him anywhere.

'Cooee! Maurice!' she cried, swinging through the tall branches of the trees. 'Come and have some of this delicious fruit I've picked.'

But there was no sign of Maurice anywhere. He wasn't climbing the creepers, or splashing in the waterfall, or teasing the grumpy old toucan. Mary asked everyone she met if they'd seen him, from the squirrels and the parrots up in the trees to the lizards and frogs in the river below. Everyone said no, but they all seemed to be laughing at her, and Mary couldn't understand why.

She soon found out, though.

'Fooled you!' giggled a voice in her ear. 'I've been on your back all the time.'

'Maurice,' said his mother, 'one more trick like that and I'm feeding you to the tigers!'

THE VAIN BUTTERFLIES

The jungle butterflies were beautiful. The trouble was, they were also very vain and never tired of boasting about their good looks.

'We are so lucky to be colourful,' the butterflies would say as they flitted from flower to flower. 'What a shame you are so plain and dull,' they would say to the elephants and monkeys.

The other animals got tired of listening to them. Then, little Fluffy the baby elephant, had an idea.

'The water in the pool is so still you can see your reflection in it,' he told the butterflies. 'Why don't you come and look?'

The butterflies flitted across the water admiring their reflection, and it wasn't long before they came just a little bit too close to the water. Once their wings were wet they found they couldn't fly. One after another, they fell into the water with a splash. The monkeys and elephants laughed as they fished out the coughing butterflies, and as for the butterflies – they kept very quiet about their beauty after that!

Tessa Tiger passed along the path to the jungle super-store. She carried a bag and a shopping list which she was reading on the way.

Suddenly, Tessa stepped on a banana skin and slipped over. In the trees above, some monkeys were munching bananas and dropping the skins.

'You should keep the jungle tidy,' called Tessa, angrily, 'and pick up anything that's dropped!'

Tessa collected the banana skins and put them in the litter-bin.

When Tessa got home from the store, she saw with dismay that her bag had a hole in it and all the fruit she had bought had dropped out on the way home! Tessa ran back along the path to find it, and saw the monkeys guzzling her shopping!

'That's my fruit!' she cried.

'Oh sorry,' replied the cheeky monkeys. 'We were just keeping the jungle tidy by picking up anything that's dropped!' And they chuckled as Tessa set off for the store for the second time that day.

Baby Monkey clung to Mummy Monkey's back as she swung through the tree-tops. To such a young monkey, the jungle seemed very big and full of mysterious noises.

'Squawwwk!' came a shrill cry which startled him.

'What's that, M . . . Mummy? ' he asked nervously, holding on to her even more tightly than before.

'Why, it's only Peter Parrot, dear,' she said, pointing as he flew past.

'Pararrrrp!' came another loud noise from somewhere far below.

'What's that, Mummy?' asked Baby Monkey again.

'Only Mister Elephant trumpeting with his trunk.' Mummy Monkey reassured him.

Next moment, a roar made Baby Monkey shiver. Before he could question his mummy about it, she rested on a branch and told him.

'That's Mister Lion calling!' she explained.

'It will take me a long time to learn so many sounds!' chattered Baby Monkey anxiously. Then he was surprised to hear one he knew straightaway.

'That's Hilda Hyena laughing,' said Mummy Monkey.

'That's the best sound!' giggled Baby Monkey, happily.

One morning, while Ned was breakfasting on a delicious green fern tree, he noticed a huge red and yellow parrot with a long orange beak staring down at him from the top branch.

'Very good morning to you!' said Ned, cheerily. 'What's your name?'

The parrot yelled with laughter and then said, 'I'm not going to talk to *you*. You're just a tiny caterpillar and all you can do is eat.'

Poor Ned was lost for words. He had never met such an unfriendly parrot, and he told his friends Charlie and Harry how mean the parrot had been to him.

That night, when the sky was pitch black, the three caterpillars crept to the fern tree. The parrot was fast asleep on a branch. Ned, Charlie and Harry began to eat all around the branch. They ate and ate and ate until they couldn't swallow another mouthful. At last, the branch broke, and the parrot fell down down to the ground and landed with a bump and a loud screech that woke the whole jungle. The trouble was, that Ned felt far too ill to laugh!

There it is again!' shouted Ferdie the Frog to his friend Liza Lizard. 'The wonderful silver ball I keep trying to catch!' And he dived into the water with a spring of his green legs.

'That's no ball,' replied Liza, darting away to her warm cave.

'That's no ball,' hissed a striped snake, slithering through the undergrowth.

'That's no ball,' chattered a troupe of monkeys, swinging home through the trees.

'That's . . . no . . . ball,' droned the sloth, hanging from a tree branch. 'That's . . . the . . . moon!'

But Ferdie was chasing silver splinters all over the pool and didn't hear him. 'I'll get it one day, Liza,' he said. 'You just wait and see!'

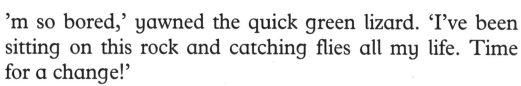

I'm so bored,' yawned the quick green lizard. 'I've been sitting on this rock and catching flies all my life. Time for a change!'

So he set off into the jungle to see how other animals lived. First, he tried hanging on a tree branch with the three-toed sloths, but he kept falling off. Then he thought he'd swing through the trees with the monkeys, but they chattered angrily at him and pelted him with nuts. Last of all, he tried hunting with the great stripey tigers. It was dreadful! The whole earth trembled with their fearful roars, and he was almost trodden underfoot by their great paws.

The quick green lizard wanted to return to his old way of life, sitting on a rock and catching flies. 'About time too!' said his mother when she saw him coming home.

RIVERBOAT RESCUE

One steamy day, beneath the scorching sun, Captain Croc O'Dile steered his riverboat towards the jetty, where Bill and Becky Baboon waited under a sunshade. Their son, Ben, whirled a thick jungle vine which he had learned to use as a lasso.

'All aboard for a gentle river trip!' cried Captain Croc O'Dile with a lazy smile.

The baboons excitedly climbed aboard but as soon as the boat had set off again, the engine failed. The boat began to drift away in the mangrove swamp . . .

'What shall we do?' they wailed. Just then, Ricky Rhinoceros passed by on the river bank, and Ben had a very clever idea . . . Using his lasso, he quickly cast its loop over the big horn on Ricky's nose, and tied the other end of the lasso to the boat. Ricky towed the riverboat back to the jetty.

'It's lucky you're so strong, Ricky!' said Ben.

'Lucky you're such an expert with a lasso!' replied Ricky, untying the loop from his horn.

'And even luckier Ben kept a cool head on such a hot day!' laughed Captain Croc O'Dile, mooring the riverboat firmly to the jetty.

Auntie Ellie was reading a story to little Edward Elephant and his friends.

'It was the dry season and the jungle waterhole was beginning to dry up . . .' she read.

'Oh! Then how did all the animals bathe?' asked Edward, sitting on her lap.

'I'll tell you later,' replied Auntie Ellie.

'It's such a fine afternoon, you should all go and play for a while.'

The youngsters agreed. Soon they were rushing happily about, playing tag, until they became very hot.

'Phew! Will you read us the rest of that story now while we cool down, please?' Edward asked Auntie Ellie.

'I've a better idea,' she said.

She told all the youngsters to put on their bathing-costumes. Then she walked to the water-hole and filled her long trunk. Hurrying back, she curled her trunk upwards and blew hard. The water sprayed out high into the air, in a great fountain and soaked the youngsters standing underneath.

'I'm glad our water-hole is full,' smiled Auntie Ellie.

'So are we!' laughed Edward.

Jack Crocodile met Harry Zebra on his way to school.

'We get the results of our maths test today,' said Harry, anxiously.

'Oh, I'm not worried,' laughed Jack. 'I always pass – one way or another.'

But when they got to school, their teacher was very cross. 'Everyone has passed the test except for Jack Crocodile. You are a very lazy animal, Jack – that is why you have failed!' she said, sternly.

'Oh dear,' said Jack, trying hard to look sad. Then, Jack yawned loudly at her, opening his mouth very wide indeed.

The teacher looked down his huge throat, with its hundreds of big, sharp teeth, and shivered in her shoes. 'Perhaps I made a mistake!' she cried. 'Why, I think you have passed after all. Well done Jack!'

Jack leaned back happily in his chair, with a lazy stretch. 'School is so easy if you're a crocodile,' he said to himself.

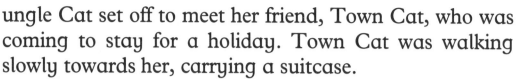

Jungle Cat set off to meet her friend, Town Cat, who was coming to stay for a holiday. Town Cat was walking slowly towards her, carrying a suitcase.

'It's a very long way to the jungle!' sighed Town Cat, wiping her brow with her paw.

'You'll feel better for a rest,' smiled Jungle Cat.

'Phew! It's very hot in the jungle!' gasped Town Cat.

'You'll soon get used to it,' replied Jungle Cat, taking her friend's suitcase.

Town Cat stared at the dense jungle all around.

'The jungle's very big, too!' she said, nervously.

At last, they reached Jungle Cat's home.

'The grass is very tall around here,' said Town Cat. 'I suppose you don't have to cut it once a week with a lawnmower, like I do back home!'

Jungle Cat smiled and, putting down the suitcase indoors, fetched her friend some home-baked banana cookies and coconut-milk shake.

Town Cat thought they tasted delicious. When she had finished them, she wiped her whiskers happily. 'M'm! It's very nice in the jungle, after all,' she said, settling back for a cat-nap in her friend's hammock.

The lion lifted his head, shook his shaggy mane and roared at the top of his voice. He made such a loud noise that a monkey dropped right out of the tree next to him with fright.

'It's still not loud enough to scare me,' said a little mouse who sat on the leaf of a palm tree next to the lion.

'What do you mean?' thundered the lion. 'That's the loudest I've ever roared. Even my father who was a champion at roaring, couldn't make that much noise.'

'Well, I'm not scared,' said the little mouse. 'You'll have to try harder. I bet I could make a noise that would scare you.'

'Don't be ridiculous, stupid mouse,' said the lion. 'No-one in the whole jungle can do that.'

'We'll see about that,' said the little mouse huffily.

The mouse drew in his breath and with all his effort he squealed at the top of his voice. The squeal was so high that human beings could not have heard it, but the lion did. It hurt his ears so much that he turned around and ran off as fast as he could through the jungle.

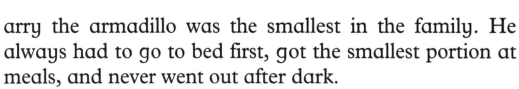

Harry the armadillo was the smallest in the family. He always had to go to bed first, got the smallest portion at meals, and never went out after dark.

'I wonder what it feels like to be a big adventurer,' he thought. 'I think it's about time I found out.' That afternoon he packed a bag with something to eat and set off into the jungle.

'I shall travel to the end of the world!' he announced proudly. He rustled off through the undergrowth until the path forked. Which way should he go? He would stop for an ant snack while he decided.

The hot sun shone down brilliantly and Harry closed his eyes. He felt tired – he must have been walking for almost half an hour! He lay down for a rest and before he knew it, he drifted off to sleep.

Harry woke with a shiver. It was beginning to get dark. What was he doing in this strange place? He must be at the end of the world!

'I don't think I like it,' he said, snuffling round to find his way back along the path.

When he was almost home, he could hear his mother and father calling him.

'Here I am. I've been to the end of world.'

'Have you indeed?' replied his mum with surprise. 'Well it's a good thing you came back by bedtime!'

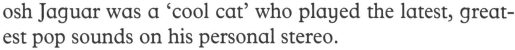

Josh Jaguar was a 'cool cat' who played the latest, greatest pop sounds on his personal stereo.

But his pride and joy was his big, bright juke-box which he had bought at a junk shop and gradually repaired so it worked perfectly.

Every time Josh pressed a different button on it, the juke-box played a golden-oldie rock-and-roll record.

One morning, Annie Ant-eater was heading back from her dance class when she heard Josh's juke-box. Annie had an idea.

'Let's have a party!' she said and Josh agreed.

They invited lots of friends and as the juke-box played everyone danced and danced.

Only when they had played every last record in the juke-box, did Josh, Annie and the others sit down to rest.

'What a great time we've had,' said Josh.

'But I'm glad we've run out of records!' puffed Annie.

Josh noticed the crimson sun rising behind the jungle as dawn approached. 'We've been dancing all night!' he chuckled. 'That must be a record, too!'

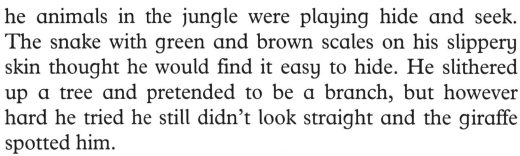

The animals in the jungle were playing hide and seek. The snake with green and brown scales on his slippery skin thought he would find it easy to hide. He slithered up a tree and pretended to be a branch, but however hard he tried he still didn't look straight and the giraffe spotted him.

'Found you!' she cried. 'Come on. Now you have to find Henrietta the Hippo with me.'

Henrietta was easy to find. Her bottom was so big that no matter where she hid, it stuck out! They discovered her straight away and together they set off to find Camilla the Chameleon.

Hide and seek was Camilla's favourite game. She had a special gift for changing her colour wherever she stood. First, she stood on a leaf and became green. Next, she jumped down on the earth and became brown. As they walked by, she jumped onto the giraffe's back and her skin took on a black and yellow pattern.

Her friends searched high and low all afternoon, but at last they gave up. 'I'm the winner!' Camilla cried from behind the giraffe's ear, but the animals never wanted to play that game again!

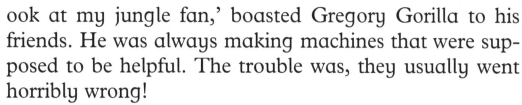

THE JUNGLE FAN

Look at my jungle fan,' boasted Gregory Gorilla to his friends. He was always making machines that were supposed to be helpful. The trouble was, they usually went horribly wrong!

Gregory proudly held up a bamboo pole, with a motor tied to it. He had fixed some large palm leaves on the top of the pole.

'The jungle is boiling hot,' said Gregory, in front of a growing crowd, 'but with my jungle fan, you can be as cool as a cucumber.'

To demonstrate, Gregory flicked the 'on' switch. The motor made the big leaves spin slowly to create a balmy breeze. Gregory was so pleased to see his new machine work, that he turned the motor onto full-power. The fan went faster and faster. Suddenly, it took off into the air, taking Gregory with it!

'Help!' he cried, as he began to rise into the tree-tops. His friends managed to catch Gregory's feet and pull him down with a bump. But the fan carried on rising, until it was quite out of sight.

'My fan isn't much use now,' Gregory told his laughing friends, 'but you are all fan-tastic!'

45

Oliver the Orang-utan sat preening himself in front of the mirror. He was very proud of his beautiful orange hair and often sat and brushed it until it glowed.

His wife looked over as she was cooking their evening supper of baked palm leaves with coconut sauce and sighed. 'You'll brush all your hair away if you're not careful,' she said.

Oliver scoffed. 'Don't be silly, dear,' he replied. 'Besides, I want to look my best if we're going out swinging later.'

His wife decided to play a trick on him . . . After dinner, Oliver decided to give his hair one last brush before they went out.

But Mrs Orang-utan had collected some orange thread. As Oliver stood brushing his hair, she dropped the pieces of thread all round his feet. When Oliver looked down, he cried, 'My beautiful hair is falling out!' But Mrs Orang-utan only laughed.

'Well, that will teach you not to spend so much time preening yourself,' she said. And it certainly did!

I'm glad I have such bright red feathers!' Red Bird said as he settled on a branch high above the jungle floor.

'My brilliant green feathers sparkle in the sun,' replied Green Bird, perched beside him.

Soon some friends flew down to join them. There were birds in every colour of the rainbow from flame-orange to mauve. They chattered and preened themselves, proudly showing off their wonderful feathers.

Shortly, another bird arrived. Her feathers were dull grey. The others hardly seemed to notice Grey Bird as they chattered and cooed.

Suddenly, Grey Bird spotted dark clouds sweeping across the sky towards them. She flapped her wings and squawked loudly to warn the others.

'A storm is coming. Quickly, find shelter!' sang Grey Bird above the chattering.

Minutes later, savage winds and rain lashed the jungle but, thanks to Grey Bird, everyone watched safely from their nests.

'You're very clever to have warned us about the storm,' Red Bird told her when it had passed. The others agreed.

'Perhaps Grey Bird is the brightest of us all!' smiled Green Bird.

HARRY'S HAMMOCK

Gina Gorilla liked weaving with jungle grasses. She made a bag for Brenda Baboon, a sun hat for Jim Giraffe, but best of all, she made an enormous hammock for Harry Hippopotamus.

He eagerly tied it between two trees. The hammock was very strong and did not break when hefty Harry climbed into it. But the trees began to bend over. The hammock slowly sank to the ground. When he climbed out, the tree-trunks straightened up again.

'I'm too heavy for a hammock,' sighed Harry.

'It's a shame not to use it,' replied Gina.

Then Harry spotted four young animals fighting over the swing in Owen Ostrich's garden. He had an idea. 'Want a go in my hammock?' he asked the youngsters.

'That's boring!' they cried. 'We're not even sleepy.'

But they didn't think it was boring when Harry persuaded them all to climb in. He pushed them as hard and as fast as he could, so that they went flying through the tree-tops and down again, whooping with delight. 'Now they can all enjoy a swing at the same time!' said Harry, who was just as glad *not* to be scraping about on the ground in his hammock.

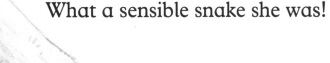

Deep in the sun-soaked jungle, a family of snakes was eagerly awaiting Aunt Polly Python's visit. The smallest snake wriggled with excitement while his sister and two older brothers kept slithering up and down a tree to see if their aunt could be seen.

'No sign of her yet!' called one.

'I'm getting tired!' replied another.

'We all are,' smiled Mummy snake. 'Let's take a little nap so we don't feel tired when Aunt Polly gets here.'

'Ho-hum! Good idea,' yawned Daddy snake.

'But if we're all asleep, there'll be no one to greet Aunt Polly,' cried the smallest snake.

Mummy smiled and told everyone exactly how to lie down. When Aunt Polly finally arrived, she looked very carefully at the sleeping snakes and laughed.

'Snakes alive!' Aunt Polly hissed happily. 'Whoever would have thought of such a clever way to give me a warm welcome, without even uttering a sound!'

Mummy snake had made her family shape themselves into letters, to spell the word 'hello'.

What a sensible snake she was!

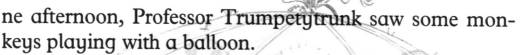

One afternoon, Professor Trumpetytrunk saw some monkeys playing with a balloon.

'Great elephant's ears!' he gasped. 'That's given me an idea!'

The professor hurried to his jungle workshop and made an enormous balloon out of some of his old socks, (which of course, were very large). He tied his huge armchair to the underside of the balloon.

'My balloon will carry me high above the jungle,' he told the monkeys the next day. 'All I have to do now is to blow up the balloon!'

The professor closed his eyes and puffed into the balloon through his trunk as hard as he possibly could. The monkeys stared as the balloon grew bigger and bigger.

'It's ready!' cried the monkeys. But the professor was puffing so hard that he didn't hear, and the balloon just carried on growing . . . . BANG! went the burst balloon, blowing Professor Trumpetytrunk into the sky *without* the help of his balloon.

When the professor came down to earth again with a bump, he cried, 'Great elephant's ears! That's given me another idea!' and the monkeys sighed . . .

Every year, the leopards held a big race to see who was the fastest hunter. 'Ready, Steady, Go!' shouted the old leopard croakily.

The young leopards sprung off to a good start. There were five of them in the race. 'You'll never beat me,' panted Lenny to his neighbour as they ran.

'I've got as good a chance as you do,' said his competitor, Leo.

'Not anymore,' said Lenny as he stuck out his front paw and tripped Leo up. Lenny managed to knock all but one of the young leopards out of the race. He was determined to win.

'Owww,' he yelped suddenly. 'Help!' He had not bargained for getting a thorn stuck in his paw. He dropped to his knees and the last leopard sprinted past him to win the race. The crowd cheered loudly, and no-one went to help Lenny. He sat and licked his wounds all on his own, and promised himself that next year he would try to win the race fairly.

Today was a very special day because Merrypen the lion, Lucy the hippopotamus and Julia the Giraffe were going to Benjamin's birthday party. Benjamin was a tiger and today he was seven years old. He had told his friends to dress in their most colourful finery.

Benjamin greeted his guests in his black sunglasses. (Black was Benjamin's favourite colour). Merrypen, Lucy and Julia gave him a black baseball cap and two pairs of black socks – one pair for his front paws and one pair for his back paws.

Benjamin began to try on all his new presents while his friends greedily tucked into the feast that he had made for them. Julia ate the yellow jelly which she kept dropping down her socks before she could reach her mouth. Lucy got her head stuck in the ice-cream bowl, and Merrypen got quite drunk on the lemonade punch which he wouldn't share with anyone.

As for Benjamin, he didn't eat anything at all, because he was such a cool cat that he didn't want to mess up his new outfit. All in all, the birthday party was a great success!

ola the gibbon lived in a safari park. She and her friends never missed the chance to tease the park-keeper whenever they could. One day, Zola was playing with some of her friends.

'Look at this,' cried George the gazelle. 'The park-keeper has been painting this old wooden fence.'

'Well, I think plain black is a bit boring,' said Zola. 'Let's brighten it up by painting some pictures on it.'

'What a good idea,' said George excitedly. 'Can I paint the first picture?'

George had only just begun to paint when the park-keeper came out of his hut.

Colin the crocodile in his fright turned around so quickly that his tail knocked George against the newly painted fence. Colin and Zola took to their heels, leaving George behind.

'You naughty zebra!' shouted the park-keeper at George. 'Just you wait 'til I catch you!'

It wasn't until George caught up with his friends that they realized why the park-keeper had thought he was a zebra – George was covered in black stripes from falling against the fence.

'Well, he'll never catch the mystery zebra now!' Zola laughed, mischievously.

Mum asked Benny the tiger to climb the ladder which lead to the loft, so that he could bring her the box of Christmas tree decorations.

'What does the box look like, Mum?' shouted Benny. 'This loft is full of boxes, and they are all covered in dust and the dust is making me sneeze . . .'

No sooner had Benny finished shouting, he felt a VERY BIG sneeze coming on.

He screwed up his wet nose, he covered his face with his paws, he even curled his tail into a knot. But it was no good. Once a sneeze decides to sneeze, not even a Bengal tiger can stop it.

It started with a tickle, then a stinging sensation right in the back of his nose. Finally the sneeze came. It was fierce and loud and made the whole tiger den shake.

'Are you all right Benny?' his mother cried, rushing up the loft ladder. 'What was that frightening noise?'

'It's OK Mum. I only sneezed,' said Benny.

'Have you found the Christmas decorations yet?'

And sure enough he had. For the box of tinsel and baubles had fallen on Benny's head when he sneezed.

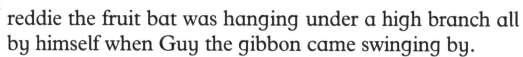

Freddie the fruit bat was hanging under a high branch all by himself when Guy the gibbon came swinging by.

'What's the matter with you?' asked Guy. 'You look down in the dumps.'

Freddie sighed. 'I'm fed up,' he said. 'All the other bats are night fliers but I hate flying in the dark – I can't see where I'm going. I'm a day bat and all my friends are asleep during the day, so I've got no-one to play with. I even have to eat my tea by myself.'

'What do you eat for tea?' asked Guy.

'Well,' said Freddie, 'I like to eat all sorts of fruits, but bananas are my favourites.'

'I love bananas!' exclaimed Guy. 'Why don't you come back with me and have tea with my family?'

And from that moment on, while the other bats were flying about in the middle of the night, Freddie was fast asleep; and when the bats finally went to bed, Freddie was just waking up, ready for a breakfast of banana sandwiches with his new friend Guy. And he never felt lonely again.

J im heard laughter as he walked through the forest. 'I wonder who that is?' he thought to himself.

Just then, three animals jumped out in front of him, laughing. 'We've been playing hide and seek,' said one of them. 'But we need a seeker. Would you like to play?'

'Yes please,' said Jim. He closed his eyes and counted to twenty. When he opened them again, the animals had all gone.

Jim looked up and down, high and low, but he couldn't find any of them. 'I give in,' he said. 'Please come out now.'

Sammy the Snake uncurled himself from the base of the tree. Peter the panther stood up from a dark rock he had been sitting on, and Paula the Parrot flew high into the sky above their heads from the brightly-coloured bush in which she had been hiding.

'Aren't we clever,' they boasted. 'We won easily! You're not very good at seeking'

But Jim just said, 'It's my turn now!' And before the animals had counted to three, Jim the chameleon had completely vanished.

Ready, steady go!' shouted Mr Growler, and the panthers sprinted off into the distance, following the leader cub.

Today was the school marathon and all the young panthers had to join in. It was also Bobby Blackcat's birthday. But however ill Bobby tried to look, and however much he limped, Mr Growler wouldn't let him off the marathon. Bobby felt very fed up, and shuffled along miserably.

In fact, Bobby felt so sorry for himself, as he mumbled and grumbled about it being the worst birthday ever, that he didn't notice the rather different path that the marathon was taking . . .

It was only when the panthers turned into the front drive of his house that Bobby looked up. There, over the door, was a banner which said, 'Happy Birthday Bobby!' And underneath the banner stood his parents with a great big chocolate cake.

'Surprise!' shouted the panthers. Even Mr Growler was there, with a large Jungle cocktail in his paw. It was the best birthday ever, and the cubs all agreed that it was *miles* better than being at school.

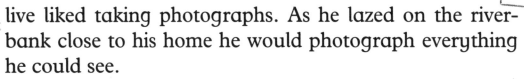

Clive liked taking photographs. As he lazed on the river-bank close to his home he would photograph everything he could see.

Click! A picture of a mangrove tree. Click! A photo of dragonflies dancing on the breeze. Click! A picture of the cool blue river as it rolled gently by. Clive would photograph anything.

One day, as he was looking for things to photograph, he saw a small lemur scampering in the branches of a nearby tree.

'I say!' Clive called. 'I'd like to snap you!'

The lemur took one look and ran away as fast as he could. After a short chase, Clive caught up with him. 'All that fuss over a photograph!' cried Clive.

'A photograph!' gasped the lemur, who was puffing and panting. 'I thought you were going to eat me. You are a crocodile after all.'

'Oh dear, perhaps I shouldn't have said snap!' Clive laughed. Of course, the lemur laughed too, very hard indeed! Clive got his picture, and the two became the best of friends from that moment on.

ebastian Hippo was taking a morning walk in the jungle. He was just trying to pass between two trees when he realized he was stuck! Sebastian bellowed and roared until his parents found him. They pushed and pulled poor Sebastian with all their might, but he didn't budge. They went to get help.

Hairy-Eared Buffalo pushed from behind. 'Ouch!' cried Sebastian. 'Your horns hurt!'

Red Bush Pig pushed from the front with his flat nose. 'Ouch!' cried Sebastian. 'That hurts!'

Stork flew over and clapped his bill. 'Cover him with mud!' he cried. So they did, but he didn't slide through.

Anhinga Bird, drying her feathers, called, 'Turn him upside down!' They tried.

A passing crane offered his help, but the crowd shouted up, 'Wrong sort of crane!'

Pelican emptied a beakful of water over Sebastian, but it didn't help.

At last, two kindly elephants arrived and quietly pulled the trees apart with their trunks.

Sebastian fell over. 'Thank you!' said the Hippo family, and they all went back to the midday mud.

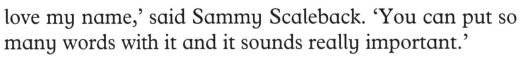

I love my name,' said Sammy Scaleback. 'You can put so many words with it and it sounds really important.'

'Like what?' asked his mother.

'Well,' said Sammy. 'Like, "I'm Sammy the Snake and I slither and slide smoothly when the sun shines".'

'That's really good,' said his mother.

Sammy went for a walk to see if he could find anyone to play with. Suddenly, he heard a shriek from above, and saw a flash of blue and gold.

'Hello,' said the strange creature.

'Hello,' said Sammy, and drawing in a deep breath he went on, 'I'm Sammy the Snake and I slither and slide smoothly when the sun shines.'

'Well, I'm Paula the Parrot, and I perch in the trees and preen my plumage.'

Sammy was astonished. 'I didn't know anyone else could talk like that!' he said. 'Let's play together and you can be my best friend.'

'Positively perfect,' said Paula.

THE PLAYGROUND

S tevie and Sophie Bushtail lived in a very quiet part of the jungle. There were no cinemas, no fairgrounds, and hardly any young squirrels. One day, as Stevie sat in a tree dropping nuts on passing buffalos, he had an idea.

'Let's build an adventure playground!' he said.

His sister thought it was an excellent plan and set to work immediately. Together, they built an obstacle course with mazes, underground tunnels, and hidden doorways. It was a squirrel's dream! When at last they had finished, Sophie said, 'Let's try it!'

They ran up the little ladder, down the tunnel, through the hole in the tree, up the pole, across the river on the swaying bridge, through the maze, and finally ended up in the tree top house. Of course, it didn't take long before news of the playground spread. Young squirrels from all over the jungle scurried to the famous obstacle course to see if they could do it, and Stevie and Sophie made hundreds of clever new friends.

Henry the sloth yawned and said to himself thoughtfully, 'What shall I do today?'

He searched around for his 'LIST OF THINGS TO DO'. 'Bother,' said Henry, 'I must have left it on Yesterday's tree.' (It was one of Henry's peculiar habits to spend each day hanging from a different tree).

The trouble was that Henry couldn't remember which tree *was* Yesterday's tree. He looked around. The jungle looked very similar in all directions.

Henry had two methods of travelling. Slowly, if he had a definite purpose, or *very* slowly if he wasn't quite sure where he wanted to go. So, moving *very* slowly, Henry began to look about him. He rolled his eyes up and down, left and right, this way and that, until he was quite exhausted. 'It's lost,' Henry sighed. 'I shall have to make a new list.' He wrote carefully the number **1** on a clean sheet of paper. 'Well that's enough for one day. I must look for Tomorrow's tree,' Henry said as he put his pen and paper away.

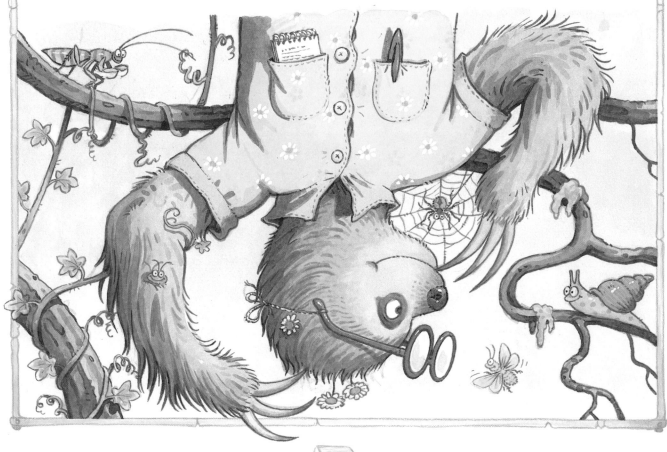

Every frog in the school was jumping about with excitement. The Frog Queen was coming to open the school sports day.

Everyone was wondering who would be this year's champion longjumper. Everyone except for one lonely frog called Fred. Fred knew that whoever won the trophy it wouldn't be *him*. He had never been any good at sports. He was such a poor jumper that he could hardly make it from one lilypad to the next.

At last, the longjump was announced. The eager competitors lined up in front of the Queen. Fred wished he was one of them and sat down feeling sorry for himself. Unfortunately, Fred sat down on a bee! The bee was so angry that it stung him on the backside.

'Yeeooww!' Fred leaped into the air. He sailed over the competitors and the Queen, over the take-off point, over the sandpit, and finally landed yards from the end of the longjump. It was a world record jump. What a hero! All the frogs cheered. They raised Fred on to their shoulders in celebration and the Queen awarded him a big gold medal.

Gina Giraffe was terrified of heights. She had never had the courage to stand up to her full height. Instead, she crawled around on all fours, stretching her neck out in front of her so as to keep her head as close to the ground as possible.

Her mother was worried – Gina was the laughing stock of the jungle. They decided to visit the oldest and wisest giraffe to ask his advice. The wise giraffe said 'Humph' and 'Humm,' and finally, 'Follow me!'

As they got deeper into the jungle, Gina began to smell the most delicious leaves just above her head. She took a bite. The young leaves were sweeter than anything she had ever tasted! Gina began to stretch her neck out to reach the higher leaves. She realized that the higher the leaves grew, the sweeter they tasted. Gina's parents gasped in amazement to see their daughter stretched out to her full height for the first time in her life, munching happily on the topmost leaves. And to this day, Gina has never again been scared of heights.

Percy the Parrot was boasting to his jungle friends. 'Look at me! Look at me!' he cried, in his terrible squeaky voice. 'How beautiful I am. Just look at my wonderful bright colours. You won't see finer plumage anywhere in the jungle.'

Although it was true that Percy was an especially colourful parrot, his friends were bored with hearing it. Night and day, jumping up and down on his perch, Percy would squawk about his fine feathers.

One morning, while Percy was busy preening himself, the other parrots crept up very quietly behind him. Percy was just admiring one blue-green wing as it caught the sunlight, when ALL the parrots let out the most incredibly loud SQUAWK!

It was so loud and unexpected that Percy leapt clean out of his feathers! He had such a fright that he didn't say a word for a week, and when his feathers finally grew back, they were completely white.

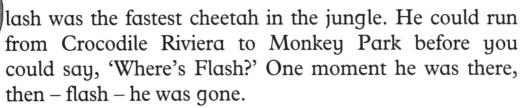

Flash was the fastest cheetah in the jungle. He could run from Crocodile Riviera to Monkey Park before you could say, 'Where's Flash?' One moment he was there, then – flash – he was gone.

Flash was also a terrible show-off. 'I'm a hundred times faster than you!' he would boast to Slowcoach the sloth. Despite all his boasting, the animals got together and made Flash a big cream cake for his birthday.

But Flash didn't want to share it, so – flash – he ate it all up and ran into the jungle. It wasn't long before Flash came crawling back to the other animals, looking quite green. 'I feel sick,' he moaned.

'It serves you right for being so greedy and running on a full stomach,' said Slowcoach. 'Come and sit with me for a while and take things easy.'

Flash and Slowcoach played chess all afternoon sitting in a tree, and Flash learned that he didn't have to rush around all the time – he could have just as much fun with his friends. And he never again ate another cream cake all by himself!

Sammy was walking along looking up at the trees. 'What are you doing?' asked Fred.

'It's Christmas tomorrow,' said Sammy, 'and the jungle looks just the same as it does all year round – no snow, no Christmas decorations. It doesn't feel like Christmas at all.'

'Well,' said Fred, 'We could do something about it.'

Fred went home and collected all the Christmas decorations which his family had not used. There were garlands of tinsel, Christmas lights and chocolates in the shape of Father Christmas.

When Sammy saw the pile of decorations that Fred had collected, he asked all the animals for their old decorations, and the whole jungle turned out to help. The giraffes draped the golden tinsel on the highest branches, the elephants threaded the Christmas lights through the forest, the tree frogs carefully hung the baubles, and the monkeys swung about putting chocolates on every branch tip. When they had finished, the whole jungle glittered with red and gold – every tree was a Christmas tree. The animals gazed in awe at the beautiful scene in front of them. On Christmas day they ate the chocolates and declared that it was the best Christmas ever.

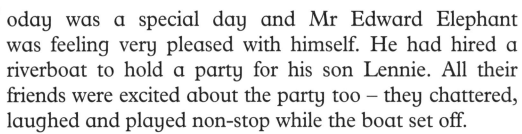

Today was a special day and Mr Edward Elephant was feeling very pleased with himself. He had hired a riverboat to hold a party for his son Lennie. All their friends were excited about the party too – they chattered, laughed and played non-stop while the boat set off.

'That's odd,' Mr Elephant thought to himself, 'one person is missing. Never mind – I can see Hattie Hippo, playing in the river on her own, so I'll ask her to join us.'

However his invitation was drowned out by a huge *SPLASSSH*. Turning around Edward could see his son waving at him from the water. Lennie had been chasing the boat on his bicycle but wobbled a little too near the river's edge. 'Oh my,' muttered Edward, 'I've been a forgetful father today and left without my son!'

Fortunately for Lennie, Chris Croc managed to rescue him with his fishing net. After which everyone partied happily into the night.

It was Kim's first day at school and she felt very shy. Her new school mates crowded around her. 'What kind of animal are you?' they asked.

'I'm a bear,' said Kim.

'We've never seen such a small bear!' hissed Snake. 'You are far too small to be a *grizzly* bear.'

'I'm a koala bear,' said Kim, fearfully.

'And you're too plain to be a *panda* bear,' snuffled Aardvark, who was quite puzzled.

'I told you – I'm a koala bear,' cried Kim, getting quite upset. But no one listened.

'You must be a *teddy* bear,' growled Alligator. At that, the animals all began to shout, 'Teddy bear! Teddy bear!'

Kim made herself as tall as she could and said, 'I may be small but I can climb the tallest trees.'

'Go on then – prove it!' jeered the others.

Kim climbed and climbed until the animals couldn't see her any more. And when she came down again, she brought some delicious honey with her. Kim was the most popular person in the class after that and no one ever mentioned her size again.

Arnold Rhinoceros loved the smell of flowers. When all his friends were out stomping through the jungle and roaring, Arnold would be just as happy gathering a posy of bright forest blooms.

Arnold's parents were worried about him. He was the laughing-stock of the jungle. The parrots made fun of him by perching on his horn, the monkeys pinched his tail and the deer tapped on his thick scaly skin, but Arnold didn't mind. He just carried on sniffing the sweet flowers and humming a pretty tune to himself.

One day, while Arnold was strolling along the river bank, he met Big Ted the tiger. *Everyone* was afraid of Big Ted. The tiger roared ferociously, and bared his huge teeth at Arnold. The animals held their breath, wondering what gentle Arnold would do. But Arnold had just taken an extra big sniff of a jungle flower, and his nose was beginning to tickle . . .

'Aatchooo!' sneezed Arnold. It was the loudest, most terrifying noise Big Ted had ever heard – and he didn't scare easily. He turned on his heels and ran off as fast as he could!

How the other animals laughed – and they *never* teased Arnold again!

ALAN ANT'S ADVENTURE

The ants of Anthill Mountain were busy collecting food. Alan was helping his friends lift a leaf, when suddenly, the twig he was standing on began to rise up into the sky taking Alan with it!

Alan peered along the twig and saw a long beak and a large eye at the other end. The twig was in a bird's mouth! Alan, (who was afraid of heights), gulped and shut his eyes.

At last, the bird came to a stop at her nest, high up in a tall tree. Alan gazed down at the ground far below. How would he ever get down there and find his way home? Alan was just about to cry, when he heard a chirpy voice.

'Hello! How did you get up here?' It was a flying squirrel. Alan told the squirrel his story.

'Don't worry!' said the friendly squirrel. 'Climb on my tail and I'll get you home. Anthill Mountain is quite near my tree.'

And so the two of them flew back down to earth, where Alan was quite a hero. After all, no ant had ever travelled on both a bird and a squirrel, all in one day!

Wind was roaring through the jungle. Trees swayed and bent their heads. Leaves and branches flew through the air. The birds and animals hid and hoped the storm would soon pass.

Hobart was a very tiny bird. He hung on to the edge of his nest as it rocked to and fro. Suddenly the branch snapped and with a terrified wail Hobart went sailing into the air.

The wind tossed him and twirled him and blew him right to the edge of the jungle. Below him lay the river.

The wind dropped poor Hobart down towards the dark water. He tried to flap his wings and fly back towards the trees, but he wasn't strong enough. He hit the water with a loud splash – and then began to rise right up into the air again! Something warm and firm was under his feet. It was Hippo's back.

Hippo had been hiding from the wind under the water and had chosen just that moment to come out and see what was happening. Just in time to save Hobart.

loth was slowly crawling along upside-down under a tree branch, minding his own business when, THUMP! something leapt onto the branch and nearly shook him off. He curled his toes tighter on the shaking branch and looked up. It was Tree-Frog.

'Come on slowcoach!' said Tree-Frog in his croaky voice. 'You'll never get anywhere going that slow. You'll never win any races! Look at me! I'll be out of sight before you've moved two paces!'

The boastful Tree-Frog hopped away, still laughing to himself. At the end of the branch he stopped to get ready for the leap to the next tree. 'Watch me, slow coach!' he shouted and leapt forward. But Tree-Frog had been so busy boasting that he didn't look where he was going and instead of landing safely on another branch he crashed into the tree trunk and fell to the ground, stunned.

When Tree-Frog came round he got to his feet and looked around him. There was Sloth, sitting in the next tree waiting. 'Sometimes,' said Sloth calmly, 'it pays to go slow.'

Tony the spotted deer noticed a tickling feeling in his antlers. He looked up and was amazed to see a little bird perched happily on the top branch of his right antler. Tony couldn't believe his eyes. Not only was the little bird chirping merrily to herself, but she also seemed to be building a nest!

'I get so bored sitting on my eggs with the same scenery to look at day after day,' Henrietta the bird said. 'This year I can sit on my eggs and you can take me with you to see lots of interesting new sights.'

Tony shouted, raged, pleaded and begged Henrietta to build her nest somewhere else but it was all in vain. She wouldn't move.

Tony carried Henrietta everywhere until her eggs hatched and at last, it was time for Henrietta and her new chicks to fly away. Strange to say, Tony was very sad to say goodbye! He made Henrietta promise to build her nest in his antlers every year. So if you ever see an antelope with a nest in his right antler, you will know for sure who he is.

THE BEAR AND THE BERRIES

Kinkajou's friend was ill and couldn't get out to find food so Kinkajou promised to bring him something to eat. He went into the jungle to gather fruit, which is what kinkajous like to eat.

Wandering through the jungle he came to a bush covered with luscious berries. He ate some himself. In fact he ate as many as his tummy would hold. Then he started to pick some to take home to his friend. The berries were small and slippery and Kinkajou wondered how he was going to carry them home to his friend without dropping any.

While he was thinking he heard a rustling behind him. It was Porcupine.

'I have an idea,' said Porcupine. 'Stick the berries on my spines and I'll walk with you to your friend's home and you can unload them there.'

So that is what they did, and a very strange sight Porcupine made walking through the jungle that day!

et's play hide-and-seek!' Christopher Crocodile said to Stripey the zebra and a little lizard called Lois. 'You both hide and I'll try to find you.'

As it was very warm, Christopher took off his jacket. He put it on a tree-stump, then closed his eyes and counted slowly to ten. Afterwards, he soon spotted Stripey behind a bush.

'It's not fair,' grumbled the zebra. 'I'm easier to find than Lois because I'm so much bigger!'

Christopher could not see Lois anywhere. He asked Stripey to help find her. But as the sun began to sink, there was still no sign of Lois although they both kept searching and calling.

'Oh! She must be lost,' said Stripey.

'We won't give up looking!' replied Christopher.

It was cooler now. He pulled on his jacket and slipped his hands into its pockets. Suddenly, Christopher gasped in surprise and carefully lifted out Lois from inside one of them.

'Found you!' he cried.

'You took your time,' yawned Lois. 'It was so cosy in there I fell asleep!'

'You were playing hide-and-sleep!' joked Stripey.

Antony the ant-eater had a problem. He hated eating ants! He quite liked flies and even worms. He loved wild mushrooms and grass with the dew still on it. Now and again he would eat a few black bugs. Sometimes the monkeys would pick bananas for him and peel them with their fast fingers. But ants! Yuck!

He felt a failure. All the animals in the jungle ate what they were supposed to eat. Giraffe browsed slowly through the jungle eating the leaves from the high branches and Sloth crawled along branches lower down and ate the leaves and fruit that grew there. Owl and Snake ate mice and small creatures and Bear ate honey and fished in the river. He was the ant-eater and he hated ants!

Antony wandered home wondering what he could do. Outside his door he saw Chimpanzee busy with a paint pot. 'There you are,' he said. 'I've solved your problem.' On the door was painted ANTONY THE ANT-HATER. 'I've changed your name!'

Geoge was playing in a clearing, happily kicking around his football, when he accidentally kicked it over a fence into a garden.

George knew that a family of porcupines owned the garden. He had heard terrible tales about them, and he was too scared to ask for his ball back. He was just walking sadly away, when a head popped over the top of the fence, and a beautiful soft voice spoke to him.

'Hello,' said the stranger. 'Is this your football?' She timidly handed the ball to George. 'I'm Penelope Prickles,' she said. 'What's your name?'

'George,' said George. 'Are you really a porcupine? My friend said you would poke me with your spikes if I spoke to you.'

'Oh no,' said Penelope. 'Porcupines only do that if they don't like someone. I thought lion cubs were fierce and would scratch me with their claws and deafen me with their roar. You don't seem like that to me. Come over the fence and we'll play football together.'

And George did just that. Later that afternoon, George and Penelope decided that lion cubs and porcupines could make very good friends after all.

Oh no!' cried Billy. 'There's only one banana left. The greedy monkeys have eaten all the rest!'

The last banana was hanging at the very top of a tall banana tree, and Billy was afraid of heights. Every time he tried to climb the long tree, he would feel dizzy, and have to climb down again.

'I'm so hungry,' grumbled Billy. 'I must reach that banana somehow.'

Just then, Jerry the giraffe came by. 'Am I glad to see you!' cried Billy.

'What's wrong, Billy?' asked Jerry, stooping his long neck down so that he could hear Billy's angry squeaks.

'I'm so very hungry, and I can't reach that banana at the top of the tree,' said Billy.

Jerry raised his long neck, took the banana between his teeth and plucked it from the tree. Bending his head down again, he gave it to Billy.

'That's what comes of having friends in high places!' said Billy, proudly.

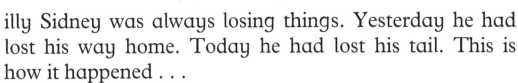

Silly Sidney was always losing things. Yesterday he had lost his way home. Today he had lost his tail. This is how it happened . . .

Silly, as his friends called him for short, had wrapped himself around the trunk of a small tree. His body was coiled round and round and his head was resting on a short branch that stuck out just below an interesting looking hole.

Silly hoped the hole might be the home of some little animal that would be nice to eat. He kept quite still and watched the hole. Nothing came out.

That was when he noticed that his tail had disappeared! He panicked! He stopped thinking about dinner. He slid his head from the branch and began to unwind himself from the tree.

Round and round he went. Lower and lower, until the last bit of him slithered along the ground. And there was his tail, right at the very end of him! Silly Sidney hadn't lost it, it had just been out of sight at the back of the tree!

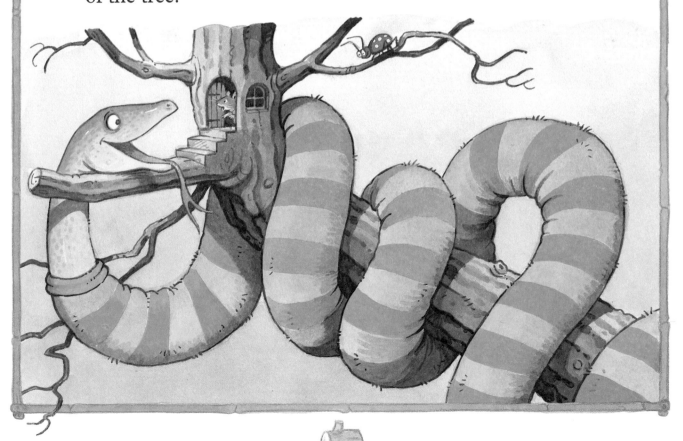

C roak! Croak!' The reeds at the edge of the jungle shivered and shook as Basil Bullfrog practised his baritone.

'Stop that horrible noise!' shouted the dragon-fly that lived near the river. 'I can't stand it any more!'

'But I have to practise,' said Basil. 'It's the concert tomorrow!'

'Well, you'll drive the audience away if *you* sing' snapped the dragon-fly, rudely. Basil sighed.

The next day all the animals gathered on the river-bank to hear the Frog Chorus. Frogs had hopped for miles to join in the concert. They sat together on the huge lilypads that grew in the river and began to sing. High and loud, soft and low they croaked and croaked and the animals on the bank swayed in time to the tunes. Suddenly a horrible, rasping 'Croak! Croak!' sounded over the singing.

'Croak! Croak!'

The animals turned to look at Basil – and saw what he had seen. Claud the crocodile was creeping up on the Frog Chorus, ready to eat them. The Frog Chorus fled! Only Basil's loud warning had saved them in time – and frightened away the crocodile!

Tiger strolled through the jungle being tigerish.

First of all, he slipped silently through the long, dried grass that was almost the same colour as his tawny coat and frightened a family of mice having a picnic.

Then he crept behind a tree and leapt out on two monkeys sitting in its shade. They shrieked with fright, jumped to their feet, crashed into each other, and finally ran off, gibbering excitedly.

He pushed his head through a bush and said 'Boo!' to an alligator lying in the shallow water at the river's edge. Alligator had just opened his mouth to have a good yawn but he gulped in a mouthful of river water instead. He was still spluttering as Tiger sneaked away.

Finally Tiger lay silently on a tree branch that stuck out over the path, until a tortoise and a lizard came by, chattering and laughing. When they were under his tree he jumped onto the ground in front of them. They were so frightened they leapt right into the air.

Tiger went home, laughing. It had been a particularly good day.

I t was carnival time in the jungle. Every year, the wise old lion would choose a new carnival king. Today, hundreds of noisy animals clamoured for his attention, each one desperate to be king for a day . . .

'I'm the best flying acrobat there ever was!' declared Rick, the spider monkey.

'But you need a sedate and dignified king – like me,' said Edgar the sloth.

'You can't change your colour though! Now *that's* what the crowd wants!' said Jerry the chameleon.

Mick the shy giraffe only watched, wondering who would be chosen. But the lion saw him standing silently behind the others and said, 'And what can *you* do?'

The other animals laughed. 'What can *he* do? Why, he's too shy to do anything!' they said.

'We'll see about that,' said the lion, angrily. 'Because he will be this year's carnival king!' At that, the lion smiled kindly at Mick, and said, 'I'm sure there's *something* you can do . . .'

And sure enough, when the king's float came by, the animals could hardly believe their eyes. For there was Mick Giraffe, in a pair of black shades and a spiked mane, but most amazing of all, he was playing the saxophone! The crowd danced and cheered. 'What a talent!' they cried. And Mick smiled proudly. He didn't feel a bit shy.

Macaw loved bright things. If he saw anything small and shiny he would pick it up and take it home to add to his collection.

One day, he was flying home with a bright ribbon he had found floating on the river, when he dropped it. Down and down it fell, right into a deep well. Macaw flew down and peered into the well. The ribbon was floating in the water. 'Oh bother!' said Macaw angrily.

Just then, Baboon came along. Macaw explained what had happened and Baboon looked down into the well. 'I can't reach it,' he said. 'But I have an idea.'

Baboon picked up a heavy stone and dropped it down the well. The water rose a little. Baboon kept on dropping stones into the water until the ribbon rose up with the water and he could reach it with his long arms. He fished it out and gave it to Macaw.

'Thank you,' said Macaw, who was very impressed. 'You're nearly as bright as my ribbon!' And he flew happily home with his treasure.

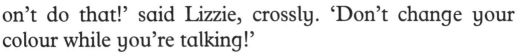

D on't do that!' said Lizzie, crossly. 'Don't change your colour while you're talking!'

'I can't help it,' said Chameleon. 'It's what I do!'

'Well I can't concentrate on what you're saying,' said Lizzie, 'and it was just getting exciting. What is this secret magic you know?'

Chameleon sighed and slowly changed a light brown colour to match the branch he was sitting on. He settled himself more comfortably and went on with his story.

'And so,' he said. 'My great, great grandfather who was called Grey Lizard, learned from a magician the secret of being invisible and from that day on, all his children and all his children's children have been able to make themselves invisible by changing the colour of their skin to match the rocks and branches and leaves they rest on. That's the secret magic!'

'Is that all?' said Lizzie (who was really rather envious of Chameleon's magic), and she slid from the branch and scuttled off home.

'Yes, that's all!' replied Chameleon as he flicked out his long tongue to catch a passing fly.

Every day, after school, Baby Koala's mother would come to collect him. He would cling on to her soft fur while she climbed high into the trees to their home. And every day, Baby Koala would watch Baby Kangaroo climb into his mother's warm pouch, and be taken home in the fastest, most exciting ride imaginable.

'Oh, how I wish I could sit in a pouch and fly through the air in great leaps!' said Baby Koala one day.

'And I wish I could be lifted up high into the tree tops,' sighed Baby Kangaroo, enviously.

'Let's swap!' said Baby Koala. And that is just what they did. When their mothers came to pick them up, it was Baby Kangaroo who held on to Koala's fur, and Baby Koala who sneaked into Kangaroo's pouch.

The trouble was, that half way up the tree, Baby Kangaroo began to feel rather afraid. As for Baby Koala, the more leaps Kangaroo made, the more ill he began to feel . . .

'Don't go any higher!' shouted Baby Kangaroo.

'Oh please stop jumping!' cried Baby Koala, at last.

And ever since then, Baby Koala is happy to cling to his mother's fur, and Baby Kangaroo is very glad to be safely tucked away in his mother's pouch again!

Lois the ring-tailed lemur was born without a single white ring on her tail. No-one knew why, but her tail was just pure black. Lois tried painting the rings on her tail. It worked very well – until she went swimming and the rings washed away. She made some bracelets to put around her tail, but they made it so heavy that she could hardly lift it. So Lois gave up trying. Instead, she decorated her tail with pretty ribbons, but she still wished for the white tail rings of the other lemurs.

One day, Lois was sunbathing in a quiet spot all by herself. She was just dozing off in the warm sun, when suddenly, Jiminy Kangaroo came leaping out of the undergrowth. 'Boo!' he said. Lois nearly jumped out of her skin! At any rate, she jumped clean out of her tail ribbons. Jiminy roared with laughter, and then, quite suddenly, stopped . . .

'Lois!' he said. 'Just *look* at your tail!' And Lois did. There were the stripes, every last one in the purest white.

'I'm a ring-tailed lemur at last!' she cried. And no-one ever really knew how Lois got the rings on her tail. I suppose it must have been the shock . . .

assie was in a temper, as usual. She crashed through the forest, leaving a trail of broken stalks and leaves behind her. She could hear the animals saying, 'There she goes again – Crosspatch Cassie!'

After a while, Cassie stopped for breath. She didn't mean to be ill-tempered. She wanted to have friends, but she was shy and awkward and that made her cross. Just then, she heard a soft whimper. Peering under a bush she saw a baby lemur looking at her with its large brown eyes. 'I'm lost!' he said.

Cassie was so surprised she forgot to be shy or bad-tempered. Instead, she bent down and carefully lifted the little lemur onto her back, and set off for his home.

The whole jungle had been searching high and low for him. You can imagine how they cheered when they saw the lost lemur arriving home on Cassie's back. Mrs Lemur hugged her, gratefully. 'Cassie,' she said, 'You're really not a crosspatch after all!'

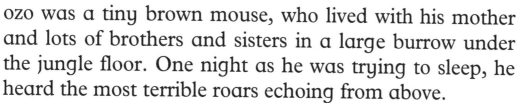

ozo was a tiny brown mouse, who lived with his mother and lots of brothers and sisters in a large burrow under the jungle floor. One night as he was trying to sleep, he heard the most terrible roars echoing from above.

Zozo crept out of the burrow and, by the light of the moon, made his way towards a dark shape in the clearing. It was Ricky the tiger, and he was rubbing his paw against a tree and groaning.

Zozo scurried up Ricky's leg and on to the huge paw. There, deep in the pad, a sharp thorn was buried. The little mouse seized it firmly in his strong teeth, and pulled, and pulled, and pulled. Pop! Out it came at last, and down Zozo fell.

'Thank you, little mouse,' said Ricky. 'Now let me take you home.'

Zozo's brothers and sisters had to rub their eyes when they saw their little brother coming home – on the back of Ricky the tiger!

Ben was a little bird who lived high in the trees on the edge of the jungle. Henry was a big hippo, who lounged lazily in the river. They weren't the sort of animals you'd think would ever meet. Until the day that Ben flew down to drink at the river, and Henry seemed an excellent perching place. Ben began to pick out all the grubs and bugs in Henry's skin. These fed Ben and made Henry very happy. It wasn't at all surprising that the two became the best of friends. If they went walking through the jungle Ben would fly above Henry, and call out to him if anything dangerous was in the way, or if someone was coming that Henry would rather not meet.

When they went on the river, Ben would sit on Henry's head while he swam slowly along. They did look a strange couple, but when the other animals saw them together, they only smiled and said, 'There go Little and Large'.

W hy Dad, why do we have a curly tail?' asked Little Boar.

'Well,' replied his father, 'it's so that our tails don't drag on the ground and get dirty.'

'Why Dad, why do we have four feet?' Little Boar went on.

'Well, we need four feet to run fast and get away from our enemies. Now why don't *you* run along and play with your friends,' said Daddy Boar, who was getting tired of all these questions.

But Little Boar wasn't satisfied. 'Why Dad, why is the jungle called the jungle?' he asked.

'Well son,' Daddy Boar sighed. 'Because it sounds like tangle, which plants in a jungle get into. Now will you please leave me in peace.'

'But why Dad, why are you called a *wild* boar?' persisted Little boar. 'I mean other animals are just squirrels, parrots or bears.'

'Stop asking me stupid questions or I will chase you and catch you up and eat you for dinner!' cried Daddy Boar in a fury.

Little Boar scampered off as fast as he could go, but at least he had the answer!

Mr Elephant was always in a bad mood when he came home from work. The animals would quake and tremble to hear his steps thudding through the jungle, and scurry away until he had passed. Until one day, a little mouse got caught in Mr Elephants path . . .

'Watch out!' he squeaked. 'You'll tread on me!'

Mr Elephant looked down at the miniature creature trembling beneath his huge foot.

'Hmph!' Mr Elephant said. 'What good is such a tiny mouse anyway?'

'Let me climb up to your ear, and I'll tell you,' said the brave mouse. So he clambered up Mr Elephant's tie, and squeaked in his ear. The animals were astonished to hear Mr Elephant roar with laughter.

'What a good joke!' giggled Mr Elephant, who already felt much better. He carried the little mouse all the way home, and made him promise to tell him a joke every day. Now, the only thing that thunders through the jungle when Mr Elephant comes home from work is his booming laughter!

Nancy was crying. The apes were holding their annual jungle ball tomorrow night. There was a prize for the best dressed, but she would not be going because she had nothing to wear.

The others were clever with their fingers. They could make beautiful dresses out of leaves and reeds, long grasses and vines. Nancy was hopeless. Whatever she made fell apart, or withered before she could wear it.

A touch as light as feathers made her stop crying. On her hand was a beautiful butterfly.

'Why are you sad?' asked the butterfly. Nancy explained.

'Just leave it to me,' said the butterfly. 'You shall be the prettiest at the ball!'

The next night, the apes gathered. They looked around for Nancy, but she was nowhere to be seen. Suddenly, everyone gasped. Into the clearing walked Nancy in a costume that shimmered and glowed with colour and beauty. No one had ever seen anything like it. For clinging to Nancy were hundreds of butterflies! And that night, Nancy won the prize.

Nina Long-Snake was getting too heavy to dangle from her favourite branches – often they snapped, and she fell to the ground and hurt herself. The doctor put her on a diet and told her to come and see him in three days time.

She moaned and groaned. She complained that she was hungry all the time, and would surely waste away to nothing if she did not eat something soon. Finally, after three days, Nina slithered off to the doctor's again.

The doctor weighed her. 'You haven't lost any weight,' he said. 'Have you stuck to the diet?'

'Of course!' wailed Nina. 'All I've eaten is one little lettuce leaf!'

The good doctor laughed. 'You are a terrible liar!' he said. 'I can see for myself what you have been eating. Is that the shape of a chocolate bar sticking out? Is that a bag of candy? And what's this lump here? Looks just like a very large slice of cake to me!'

'I never get away with anything,' grumbled Nina as she slithered home again on a second diet.

The crocodile was dozing by the river in the soft oozy mud, warming his scaly body, when a little bird fluttered down to have a drink in the river.

'Ahem, er, excuse me, but this is such a perfect day, is it not?' smiled the crocodile, trying not to bare his teeth.

'Oh yes, it is beautiful,' said the bird.

'It would be the most perfect day of my life, if only I didn't have this little stone caught between my teeth. You birds are so lucky not having teeth, you really have no idea of how uncomfortable it is.' He opened his large jaws and said, 'Can you see it?'

'No, I'm afraid not,' said the little bird.

'Come closer and you may be able to pick it out with that clever little beak of yours.' But the little bird was not so foolish. Instead of hopping into those gloomy gaping jaws himself, the bird rolled a stone into the crocodile's mouth. 'SNAP!' went the crocodile's teeth, right onto the stone. 'Aargh!' roared the wicked crocodile.

'How's your toothache now?' laughed the little bird, as he flew away.

THE LAST LAUGH

Osborne the Parrakeet was the jungle comedian. There was no end to his little jokes, pranks and impressions. He impersonated Sloth running a race, he made jokes about Alligator's false teeth, and told the story of Rhinoceros's unsuccessful diet. The trouble was, that after a while, Osborne's little act wasn't funny anymore. In fact, it made some animals VERY angry indeed!

'Can't you take a joke?' chirped Osborne.

'No!' they growled. The animals decided to give Osborne a taste of his own medicine. When he went to sleep on his perch one night, the monkeys scurried up Osborne's tree, and neatly tied his wings together.

The whole jungle gathered together under Osborne's tree to watch the spectacle! And sure enough, when Osborne woke, he took off from his perch to fly down to the ground and in mid air, he realized he could barely fly at all! Osborne shrieked in horror. Luckily for him, the animals had fixed a net under his perch. Osborne landed gently and bounced up into the air again, chirping furiously.

'Can't you take a joke?' they laughed. And Osborne was very careful who he joked about after that!